CLASSICS Illustrated®

Herman Melville
MOBY DICK

essay by
Debra Doyle, Ph.D.

ACCLAIM BOOKS
STUDY GUIDE

Moby Dick

adaption by Albert L. Kanter
art by Louis Zansky

Classics Illustrated: Moby Dick © Twin Circle Publishing Co.,
a division of Frawley Enterprises; licensed to First Classics, Inc.
All new material and compilation © 1997 by Acclaim Books, Inc.

Dale-Chall R.L.: 7.55

ISBN 1-57840-013-9

Acclaim Books, New York, NY
Printed in the United States

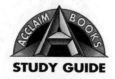

STUDY GUIDE

OUT OF THE BLEAK DECEMBER DUSK, WALKS THE LONE FIGURE OF *ISHMAEL*, LOOKING FOR A NIGHT'S LODGING...

SPOUTER INN? PETER COFFIN? RATHER OMINOUS! OH WELL,-I MIGHT- BUT ON SO COLD A NIGHT, ANY SHELTER WILL DO!

CAN YOU PUT UP ONE MORE FOR THE NIGHT?

SORRY, M LAD, BUT I'M FULL UP!

I'M WILLING TO TAKE ANYTHING. HOW ABOUT IT?

WELL, IF YOU CARE TO BED WITH A HARPOONEER, I'LL SHOW YOU YOUR PLACE.

QUITE A CLIMB...ER, THIS HARPOONEER... WHERE IS HE?

PROBABLY SELLING HIS HEAD!

COME, NOW! I MAY LOOK GREEN, BUT DON'T LET MY APPEARANCE FOOL YOU!

SO YOU DON'T BELIEVE ME, EH? WELL, YE SHALL SEE!

HERE IS YOUR ROOM. GOOD NIGHT!

I WONDER WHAT HE MEANT BY "YE SHALL SEE"? OH WELL. I MAY AS WELL GET SOME SLEEP!

SUDDENLY THE DOOR OF THE ROOM SWINGS OPEN, AWAKING ISHMAEL...

WHAT WAS THAT?

A LARGE, DARK, EERIE FIGURE PROCEEDS TO THE CHEST AND BRINGS FORTH A SMALL IDOL AND...A HUMAN HEAD...

A CHANTING PRAYER BEGINS

THEN THE STRANGELY GARBED MAN TURNS

GULP!

SUDDENLY, HE NOTICES ISHMAEL...

WHO-E-DEBEL YOU? GET OUT MY BED, OR I KILL 'EE!

HELP! LANDLORD— SAVE ME, QUICK!

GET HIM AWAY FROM ME, *WILL YOU!!*

WHAT TH'! - HEY, QUEEQUEG, *STOP IT!* THAT'S YOUR NEW ROOM-MATE!

ROOM-MATE? I TOUGHT HE WAS TIEF!

(PUFF-PUFF) CONFOUND IT. WHY DIDN'T YOU TELL ME (PUFF) THE HARPOONEER WAS A CANNIBAL?

HA, HA. DON'T WORRY, QUEEQUEG WON'T HARM A HAIR ON YOUR HEAD!

THE NEXT MORNING AT BREAKFAST

GRUB HO!

GOOD! I'M SO HUNGRY I COULD EAT A BULL.

AHHH, BREAD!

MAYBE WANT BREAD-MAYBE?

YES, THANKS.

AHH . . . IT'S GOOD HERE, QUEEQUEG! SAY . . . I HOPE YOU WON'T MIND MY BUNKING WITH YOU AGAIN.

OH, YA, I LIKE VER' MUCH TO.

THAT EVENING . . .

SAY, QUEEQUEG, HOW DO YOU EXPECT TO SHAVE IF YOU HAVEN'T A RAZOR?

I USE HARPOON . . . MUCH MORE SHARP THAN RAZOR

QUEEQUEG, EACH TIME I SEE YOU, YOU AMAZE ME MORE AND MORE!

WE VER' GOOD FRIENDS. NO, ISHMAEL?

WHY, YES! WHY DO YOU ASK?

IN MY COUNTRY, ALL GOOD FRIENDS RUB HEADS TOGETHER AND BECOME BLOOD BROTHERS. IS IT ALL RIGHT WITH YOU IF WE DO SAME?

WHY, OF COURSE IT IS!

ALL BLOOD BROTHERS SHARE EVERYTHING . . . HERE, TAKE HALF MY SILVER.

B-BUT!

GOLLY, LOOK- HE'S REALLY GIVING IT TO HIM!

WELL I'LL BE!

BY GOL', ALMOST FORGET . . . WAIT HERE MINUTE

I WONDER WHERE HE WENT?

HERE YOU ARE. 'EES MY GREATEST TREASURE!

FORSOOTH, 'TIS GOOD OF YOU, QUEEQUEG. BUT YOU REALLY SHOULDN'T DO THIS FOR ME!

IT IS BEAUTIFUL-NO?

GULP-I-I-IT SURE IS!

And so-- a strange friendship arises between the harpooning cannibal, Queequeg, and the seaman, Ishmael. Together they set forth in the quest of Adventure!

WHAT SORT OF NONSENSE IS THIS? A WHITE MAN BEFRIEND-ING A SAVAGE?

ISHMAEL . . . I NO UN'ERSTAN' WHY PEOPLE NO LIKE OUR FRIEN'SHIP?

FOLKS ARE STRANGE QUEEQUEG. THEY PREACH EQUALITY, BUT RARELY PRACTICE IT-WELL, WE'RE APPROACHING THE SHIP!

THIS IS OUR FIRST VOYAGE TOGETHER, QUEEQUEG, AND WE'RE HEADING FOR NAN-TUCKET!

ALL RIGHT, MEN. SNAP INTO IT! WE'RE LEAVING IN A FEW MINUTES!

THE MOSS

THE MOSS SOON CASTS OFF-

GET A WHIFF OF THE SEA AIR.

YAAAH.

LOOK AT THAT FUNNY LOOKING GINK, BOYS!

WHERE DID HE FIND THAT FACE!

THEY MAKE FUN FROM QUEEQUEG. KEEP *SHUT UP!*

AND THAT HAIR STYLE! *HA-HA*

COME ON, QUEEQUEG. YOU'VE GOT TO MAKE IT!

THEY'RE GONE!

LOOK ON, YOU HARDIES-- HE'S GOT IT . . . HE GRABBED THE LIFE SAVER!

I NEVER THOUGHT YOU'D MAKE IT, YOU OLD CODGER. COME ON, LET ME GIVE YOU A HAND.

BRRRRR-QUEEQUEG FEEL COLD.

CARRY HIM CAREFULLY!

YE BLASTED BARNACLE! I SHOULD REALLY LOCK YOU IN THE BRIG, BUT YE DESERVE A GOLD MEDAL INSTEAD!

I DON'T KNOW WHAT TO SAY . . . I WANT TO APOLOGIZE FOR CALLING YOU ALL THOSE NAMES . . .I-I-I-

EET WAS NOTHING-- FORGET EET!

FROM ONE TRANQUIL SUNSET TO ANOTHER, THE MOSS SAILS ON TO ITS FINAL DESTINATION AT NANTUCKET!

Chapter II
"The Pequod & Captain Ahab"

SHIPMATES, HAVE YE SIGNED WITH THAT SHIP?

AYE-SO WHAT?

SOLD YOUR SOULS TO THE DEVIL, THAT'S WHAT!

COME NOW, MAN, WHAT KIND OF A FABLE ARE YOU GIVING ME?

METHINKS YE NEVER HEARD OF OLD THUNDER?

NO, WHO IS HE?

CAPTAIN AHAB, *YOUR* SKIPPER, IS THE WORST THIS SIDE OF HADES. YOU PROBABLY NEVER HEARD OF HOW HE WILLED UPON HIMSELF THE CURSE OF THE ALTAR OF SANTA, AND LOST HIS LEG THEREBY.

I'M A GOD-FEARING MAN, BUT I DON'T BELIEVE IN SUCH NONSENSE!

YOU THINK I'M CRAZY, DON'T YOU? WELL, YOU'LL LEARN . . . GOOD DAY, GENTLE-MEN!

I THINK HE REALLY MUST BE CRAZY . . . BUT I WONDER . . .

FO'GET HEEM. LET US HAVE FUN.

Y-YES, LET'S.

SOON THE PEQUOD IS FULLY RIGGED AND SUPPLIED. EARLY ONE MISTY MORNING, QUEEQUEG AND ISHMAEL SET OUT TO BOARD HER, READY FOR THE LONG VOYAGE WHICH LIES AHEAD.

CROSS A NORTHERN ROUTE IT SAILS, THIS STRANGE SHIP, HEADED BY A YET UNSEEN MASTER. AN INVISIBLE FORCE GUIDES THE CREW IN THEIR PURSUIT OF THE GIGANTIC MAMMALS OF THE DEEP . . . WHALES! STRANGE INDEED . . . AND STRANGE, TOO, ARE THE MEN OF THE CREW . . .

Starbuck
CHIEF MATE

A QUAKER BY DESCENT, LONG, HARD AS NAILS AND POWERFUL - DEEPLY RELIGIOUS AND STAID, HE GUIDES HIS MEN THROUGH THEIR PERILS WITH A SILENT, CAREFUL COURAGE.

STUBB
SECOND MATE

EASY GOING, AND FEARLESS, HAPPY-GO-LUCKY IN HIS ATTITUDE TOWARD WHALES. HIS PIPE, BEING JUST AS MUCH A PART OF HIS REGULAR FEATURES AS HIS NOSE.

Flask
THIRD MATE

SHORT AND STOUT, FLASK IS VERY PUGNACIOUS CONCERNING WHALES . . . NICKNAMED "KING-POST" BY THE MEN, THE TASK OF KILLING WHALES IS JUST SO MUCH FUN TO HIM.

Queequeg
STARBUCK'S SQUIRE

A PURE-BLOODED, GAY-HEADER INDIAN. HE GAVE UP THE SAFETY OF DEER HUNTING IN THE WILDS OF NEW ENGLAND FOR THE DANGERS OF HARPOONING WHALES IN THE BROAD ATLANTIC.

Tashtego
STUBB'S SQUIRE

A PURE-BLOODED, GAY-HEADER INDIAN. HE GAVE UP THE SAFETY OF DEER HUNTING IN THE WILDS OF NEW ENGLAND FOR THE DANGERS OF HARPOONING WHALES IN THE BROAD ATLANTIC.

Daggoo
FLASK'S SQUIRE

A GIGANTIC, COALBLACK NEGRO, WITH A LION-LIKE TREAD. HOOPS ARE SUSPENDED FROM HIS EARS LIKE RING BOLTS. WHEN TOGETHER, FLASK LOOKS LIKE A CHESSMAN BESIDE HIM.

Fedallah
MYSTERIOUS STRANGER

THIS ORIENTAL BOARDED THE SHIP OUT OF THIN AIR. THE MEN NEVER SEE MUCH OF HIM, EXCEPT WHEN HE IS AT AHAB'S SIDE IN THE THICK OF BATTLE WITH A WHALE.

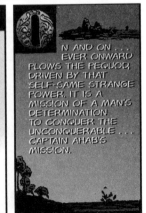

N AND ON . . . EVER ONWARD PLOWS THE PEQUOD, DRIVEN BY THAT SELF-SAME STRANGE POWER. IT IS A MISSION OF A MAN'S DETERMINATION TO CONQUER THE UNCONQUERABLE . . . CAPTAIN AHAB'S MISSION.

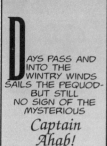

DAYS PASS AND INTO THE WINTRY WINDS SAILS THE PEQUOD- BUT STILL NO SIGN OF THE MYSTERIOUS

Captain Ahab!

SUDDENLY, ONE DAY . . .

QUICK, QUEEQUEG, LOOK!

CAPTAIN AHAB!

OLD THUNDER HIMSELF!

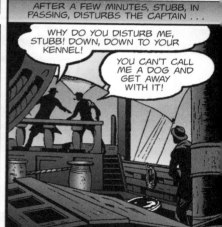

AFTER A FEW MINUTES, STUBB, IN PASSING, DISTURBS THE CAPTAIN . . .

WHY DO YOU DISTURB ME, STUBB! DOWN, DOWN TO YOUR KENNEL!

YOU CAN'T CALL ME A DOG AND GET AWAY WITH IT!

THEN I'LL *CALL* YOU A *MULE AND A PIG, TEN TIMES OVER!*

NOW GET!

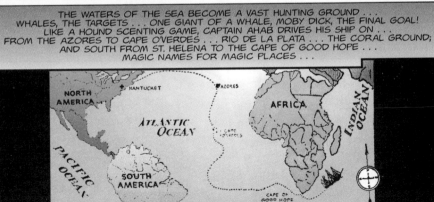

THE WATERS OF THE SEA BECOME A VAST HUNTING GROUND...
WHALES, THE TARGETS... ONE GIANT OF A WHALE, MOBY DICK, THE FINAL GOAL!
LIKE A HOUND SCENTING GAME, CAPTAIN AHAB DRIVES HIS SHIP ON...
FROM THE AZORES TO CAPE O'VERDES... RIO DE LA PLATA... THE CORAL GROUND;
AND SOUTH FROM ST. HELENA TO THE CAPE OF GOOD HOPE...
MAGIC NAMES FOR MAGIC PLACES...

I'LL NEVER LIVE THROUGH THESE STORMS QUEEQUEG! CAPE OF GOOD HOPE THEY CALL THIS PLACE! THEY SHOULD RENAME IT CAPE *FORLORN!*

SHH! CAP'N AHAB MAY NOT LIKE TO HEAR THAT.

AHAB THIS . . . AHAB THAT! HE'S NOT A MAN - HE'S A DEVIL WITHOUT FEAR. OOF! - WELL, WHAT ARE YOU LAUGHING AT!

HA HA! YOU LOOK VER' FUNNY . . . MAYBE SOON YOU FLY!

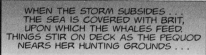

WHEN THE STORM SUBSIDES . . . THE SEA IS COVERED WITH BRIT, UPON WHICH THE WHALES FEED. THINGS STIR ON DECK AS THE PEQUOD NEARS HER HUNTING GROUNDS . . .

THAR SHE BLOWS!

WHET YOUR APPETITES, MEN! YE'LL NEED STRONG, LEATHER STOMACHS WHEN YE COME TO THE WHITE WHALE!

EASY MEN. DON'T LET AHAB EXCITE YOU! BUT WHEN YOU DO BEGIN, ROW ON LIKE THUNDERCLAPS! THAT'S ALL!

TOW IN THE PRIZE, MY HARDIES, BUT BE EASY ON ITS CARCASS!

IT GIVES ME AN APPETITE. PASHTEGO, CUT ME A STEAK FROM ITS TENDER HIDE!

AT THE SIGN OF BLOOD, DOZENS OF SHARKS BEGIN RAVAGING THE BODY OF THE WHALE.

LOOK AT THEM CRITTERS EAT! I SURE WOULDN'T LIKE TO BE DOWN THERE!

A PRETTY DISH YOU'D MAKE!

THEN THE TASK OF CUTTING THE WHALE BEGINS . . .

A HUGE HOOK, LASHED TO THE MAIN MAST IS SUSPENDED THROUGH A HOLE CARVED NEAR THE WHALE'S TAIL, AND A LARGE SEMI-CIRCULAR INCISION IS MADE AROUND THIS HOLE WITH A CUTTING SPADE . . .

THE CREW, STRIKING UP A WILD CHORUS, COMMENCES HEAVING AT THE WINDLASS . . .

THE SHIP CAREENS AT ITS SIDE AS THE WHALE'S WEIGHT TUGS IT OVER . . .

SUDDENLY A LOUD RIP IS HEARD. THE PEQUOD RIGHTS ITSELF, AND A CHEER ARISES. THE TACKLE STARTS STRIPPING THE BLUBBER . . .

JUST AS IN PEELING AN ORANGE, THE BLUBBER COMES OFF IN ONE STRIP . . .

ANOTHER HOLE IS MADE IN THE HEAVY END. THEN EXPERT SWORDSMEN SEVER THE WHALE IN TWO . . .

THE BLUBBER IS THEN REMOVED TO THE BLUBBER ROOM, AND COILED BY MANY HANDS.

HAUL IN THE CHAINS! TIE ITS HEAD TO THE LARBOARD, AND LET ITS CARCASS GO ASTERN!

LOOK, QUEEQUEG. SEE THOSE VULTURES DEVOURING THE WHALE'S PEELED WHITE BODY . . . NOT A PLEASANT SIGHT, EH?

THE PEQUOD

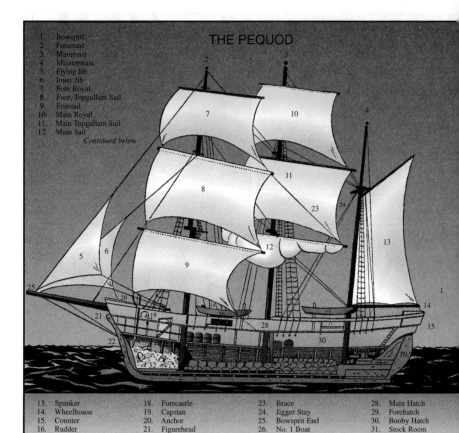

1. Bowsprit
2. Foremast
3. Mainmast
4. Mizzenmast
5. Flying Jib
6. Inner Jib
7. Fore Royal
8. Fore, Topgallant Sail
9. Foresail
10. Main Royal
11. Main Topgallant Sail
12. Main Sail
Continued below

13.	Spanker	18.	Forecastle	23.	Brace	28.	Main Hatch
14.	Wheelhouse	19.	Capstan	24.	Jigger Stay	29.	Forehatch
15.	Counter	20.	Anchor	25.	Bowsprit End	30.	Booby Hatch
16.	Rudder	21.	Figurehead	26.	No. 1 Boat	31.	Stock Room
17.	Galley	22.	Cut Water	27.	No. 2 Boat	32.	Blubber Room

Whales are the largest of animals and belong to the Pelagic species (they inhabit the deep seas far from land).

Of the two distinct types, the **RIGHT WHALE** (Balatna Mysticetus) is the smaller but most valuable. A 50 foot specimen of these huge mammals may yield 200 to 300 barrels of shale-oil, and from his head, from 1 to 2 tons of precious whalebone. It is usually found in the North Atlantic and Arctic Oceans, and it feeds primarily on Brit, a yellow vegetation which floats.

The **SPERM WHALE** (Physeter Macrocephalus), larger and fiercer, becomes a killer when attacked. Its spermoil has great commercial value. Its intestines frequently yield Ambergis, used in making very expensive perfumes. The **SPERM WHALE** floats with its buoyant head high above the waters. Its lower jaw has great conical teeth and it feeds largely on Squids, swallowing great pieces at a time. A native of the South Seas and warmer waters.

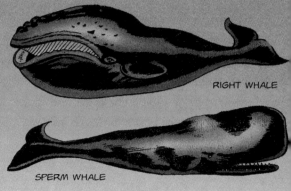

RIGHT WHALE

SPERM WHALE

THE STRICKEN WHALE, CRAZED WITH PAIN, RUSHES HEADLONG FOR THE PEQUOD.

WATCH OUT! IT'S HEADING FOR THE SHIP!

BUT A SCHOOL OF SHARKS, SMELLING BLOOD, PURSUES THE WOUNDED MONSTER . . .

AYE, THE SHARKS SURE MADE QUICK WORK OF HIM!

FLASK! WONDER WHAT THE OLD MAN WANTS WITH THE FOOL HEADS OF THESE LEVIATHANS?

HAVEN'T YOU HEARD THAT A BOAT NEVER CAPSIZES WITH THE HEAD OF A SPERM WHALE ON THE STARBOARD SIDE, AND THAT OF A RIGHT WHALE ON THE LARBOARD?

HOW DO YOU KNOW?

I HEARD THIS ORIENTAL GHOST OF FEDALLAH SAY SO!

FEDALLAH! HE'S A STRANGE ONE. I THINK, FLASK, HE'S THE DEVIL IN DISGUISE. HAVE YE NOTICED HOW HE URGES AHAB ON HIS MAD HUNT FOR MOBY DICK?

AYE, I HAVE. AND DID YOU SEE THE STRANGE WAY HE CAME ABOARD! DIDN'T SIGN UP LIKE THE REST OF US. HE CAME ON SHIP, OUT OF THIN AIR!

TIME WILL TELL WHAT HE REALLY IS, BUT I CAN TAKE AN OATH NOW, HE'S A DANGEROUS ONE!

AFTER THE WHALE HAD BEEN HARNESSED TO THE SHIP, TASHTEGO DEFTLY SWINGS DOWN UPON ITS HEAD, CUTS A HOLE IN IT, AND THEN COMES THE PROCESS OF REMOVING THE MILKY OIL.

YOU CAN START LOWERING BUCKETS, BOYS!

INTO THE TUN YOU GO!

SOON BUCKET UPON BUCKET COME UP WITH THEIR GLISTENING CONTENTS.

TAKE IT AWAY!

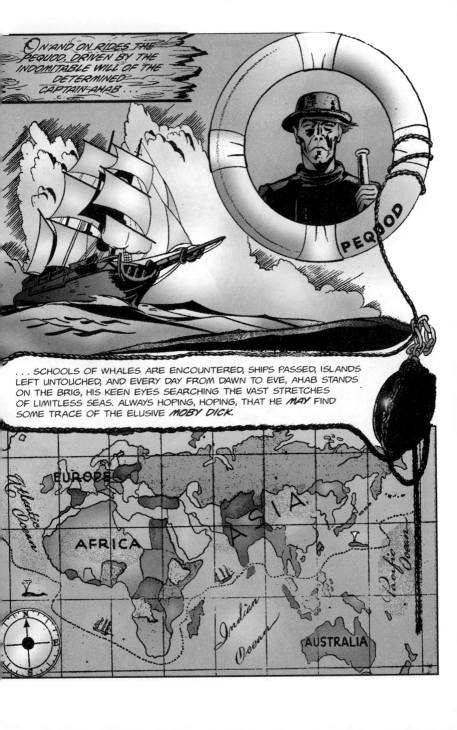

ON AND ON RIDES THE PEQUOD, DRIVEN BY THE INDOMITABLE WILL OF THE DETERMINED CAPTAIN AHAB...

PEQUOD

... SCHOOLS OF WHALES ARE ENCOUNTERED, SHIPS PASSED, ISLANDS LEFT UNTOUCHED, AND EVERY DAY FROM DAWN TO EVE, AHAB STANDS ON THE BRIG, HIS KEEN EYES SEARCHING THE VAST STRETCHES OF LIMITLESS SEAS. ALWAYS HOPING, HOPING, THAT HE *MAY* FIND SOME TRACE OF THE ELUSIVE *MOBY DICK*.

SHOULD I CUT HIM LOOSE?

PLEASE, BOSS, DO!

I'D MUCH RATHER YOU CUT OUT HIS PASTY INNARDS THAN LOSE THAT WHALE . . . *CUT HIM LOOSE!!*

MEANWHILE . . . THE ANGRY WHALE SNEAKS UP BEHIND THE BOAT, AND SLAPS IT WITH ITS TAIL . . . AND POOR PIP AGAIN FINDS HIMSELF IN A PRECARIOUS POSITION . . .

STICK TO THE BOAT, PIP, OR BY GOLLY, I'LL LET YOU REMAIN IN THE OCEAN!

YOW, SUH!

HELP! HELP!

I'M A MAN OF MY WORD. IN THE WATER YOU'LL REMAIN!

BUT STUBB DOESN'T SEE THE SHARKS NEAR BY . . .

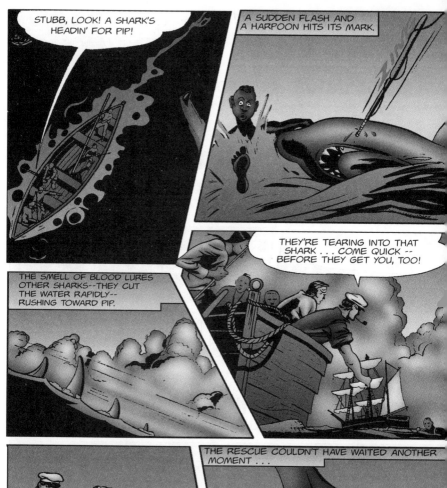

STUBB, LOOK! A SHARK'S HEADIN' FOR PIP!

A SUDDEN FLASH AND A HARPOON HITS ITS MARK.

THE SMELL OF BLOOD LURES OTHER SHARKS--THEY CUT THE WATER RAPIDLY-- RUSHING TOWARD PIP.

THEY'RE TEARING INTO THAT SHARK . . . COME QUICK -- BEFORE THEY GET YOU, TOO!

THE RESCUE COULDN'T HAVE WAITED ANOTHER MOMENT . . .

AYE, AYE, CAPTAIN. LET'S SHAKE BONES TOGETHER; AN ARM THAT CAN NEVER SHRINK, AND A LEG THAT CAN NEVER RUN!

TELL ME ABOUT THE WHITE WHALE! DID HE TAKE THAT ARM OFF A' YOU?

AYE, THAT HE DID!

SPIN ME THAT YARN. HOW WAS IT?

I MET HIM LAST SEASON ON THE LINE TO THE EAST. A GREAT MILKY HUMP OF A WHALE, ALL CROWS FEET AND WRINKLES -- WITH HARPOONS STICKIN' OUT HIS STAR-BOARD FIN.

AYE. THAT WAS *HE*, AND THOSE WERE *MY* HAR-POONS!

"WELL, THIS GREAT WHALE RUNS ALL AFOAM TO THE POD, AND GOES SNAPPING FURIOUSLY AT MY FAST LINE . . ."

"BUT IN THE BITING, THE LINE CAUGHT IN HIS TEETH. TAKING ADVANTAGE OF THIS, I LEAPT INTO MY FIRST MATE'S BOAT . . ."

. . .AND PROCEEDED TO HARPOON HIM. . ."

"BUT DOWN CAME HIS TAIL, CUTTING THE BOAT IN HALF. I, AT THAT MOMENT, RELEASED MY IRON."

"HE FREED HIMSELF AND CARRIED ME TO THE SEA. SUDDENLY, THE BARB OF THE SECOND IRON CAUGHT MY ARM, AND BORE ME DOWN TO HELL'S FLAMES . . ."

AND SEARED ITS WAY THROUGH MY FLESH -- AND SO HERE I AM. LET BUNGER, SHIP'S SURGEON, TELL YOU THE REST!

NOTHING MUCH TO SAY -- EXCEPTING I'M QUITE SUPRISED THE CAPTAIN STILL LIVES! DRINK?

HA-HA! THAT'S BUNGER FOR YOU. HE SAYS SOME THING, AND DRINKS A TOAST TO IT! HE'S A GOOD DOCTOR, THOUGH. SAVED MY LIFE HE DID!

WELL, HAVE YOU SEEN MOBY DICK SINCE?

YES, TWICE. BUT I NEVER TOUCHED HIM. AIN'T ONE LIMB ENOUGH? BUT I SUPPOSE YOU WILL TRACK HIM DOWN FOR THE MAGNET THAT HE IS.

AYE, THAT, I WILL!

Chapter III
"Moby Dick"

I'M SORRY, BUT . . .

BACK ON DECK! OR DO I HAVE TO SHOOT?

AYE, AYE, SIR!

FOR AN HOUR, CAPTAIN AHAB STANDS AS THOUGH IN A TRANCE . . .

COME IN!

KNOCK KNOCK

SLAM

BEG PARDON, SIR. BUT QUEEGQUEG, THE HARPOONEER, IS DOWN WITH A FEVER!

IT'S ONE THING OR ANOTHER! *BLAST IT!* WHAT DO YOU WANT ME TO DO?

WELL, I THOUGHT, SIR --

WELL, STOP YOUR THINKING. HE SHOULD HAVE TAKEN SICK FOUR HOURS BEFORE. THE SHIP WE MET THEN HAD A SURGEON!

ISHMAEL RETURNS TO THE HOLD.

ISHMAEL, ISHMAEL! I FEEL LIKE, MAYBE TOTO BECKONS!

COME NOW, QUEEQUEG. DON'T BE SO PESSIMISTIC!

BUT -- I'M DYING. PLEASE ASK CARPENTER TO MAKE ME COFFIN!

AH! POOR FELLOW. IF HE HAS A COFFIN, HE'LL HAVE TO DIE!

COULD YOU MAKE A COFFIN?

MAY THE LORD SAVE ME! A COFFIN . . . IT'S PAST THE HOUR AHAB GAVE ME TO FINISH HIS LEG!

AM I TO MAKE MY OWN COFFIN?

NO, NO! IT'S FOR QUEEQUEG!

THE NEXT MORNING . . .

HUH? WHAT'S THIS?

QUEEQUEG!!! HOW COME YOU'RE UP?

ME? I FEEL GOOD NOW!

MOVE OVER! I'M GETTING OUT OF HERE!

Y!!! IT'S A GHOST!

LOOK AT THAT SAVAGE! ONLY A CANNIBAL WOULD RECUPERATE IN ONE DAY!

AND DID YOU HEAR? HE IS MAKING A CHEST OUT OF HIS COFFIN!

AS THE PEQUOD MOVES AHEAD, OUT OF THE EAST ROLLS THE HORROR OF ALL SEAMEN . . . THE TYPHOON!

LASH THE BOATS!

TOO LATE! AHAB'S BOAT IS SMASHED!

THE RODS, THE RODS. DROP THEM OVERBOARD, FORE AND AFT!

LOOK ALOFT. THE CORPOSANTS!

BLAST IT! THE CORPOSANTS! . . . HAVE MERCY ON US ALL!

AYE, AYE, MEN. MARK IT WELL. THE WHITE FLAME LEADS US TO THE *WHITE WHALE!*

YOUR BOAT!! LOOK AT YOUR BOAT!

FLASHING LIGHTNING STRIKES, AND THE HARPOONS BLAZE WITH HEAVEN'S ELECTRICITY!

GOD IS AGAINST YOU. 'TIS AN ILL VOYAGE!

HE NEXT MORNING

OH! THE FAIR WIND!
OH-YE-HO!
CHEERY MEN!

THERE HE LIES, SLEEPING. OH LORD, IF ONLY I HAD THE COURAGE TO WREST THE POWER FROM HIS LIVING HANDS!

THE RIFLE!

STARBUCK!

YES, SIR!

WHAT TIME IS IT?

TWELVE BELLS, SIR! -- TIME TO AWAKEN . . . PHEW . . . !

AHAB GOES UP ON DECK. WHAT SHIP IS IT?

IT'S THE RACHEL, SIR!

HAVE YOU SEEN THE WHITE WHALE?

AYE, YESTERDAY . . . HAVE YOU SEEN A WHALE BOAT ADRIFT ?

WHERE IS THE WHALE? NOT KILLED? NOT KILLED?

NO - SHE HASN'T BEEN KILLED.

THEN QUICK, TELL ME WHAT HAPPENED, ...HASTEN!

YESTERDAY, WE SIGHTED A SHOAL OF LEVIATHANS AND WE PURSUED THEM. SUDDENLY, THE HUGE HUMP AND HEAD OF A WHITE MONSTER LOOMED AHEAD...

GO ON!

MY NUMBER FOUR BOAT, THE SWIFTEST, SUCCEEDED IN FASTENING TO THE WHITE WHALE. THEN...A SUDDEN FLASH...THE MONSTER SURGED FORWARD... AND, IN THE DISTANCE, ALL THAT COULD BE SEEN WAS THE DIMINISHED, DOTTED BOAT, THE A SWIFT GLEAM OF BUBBLING WHITE WATER, AND AFTER THAT, NOTHING MORE...
SOB - SOB -

WHAT DO YOU WANT ME TO DO ABOUT IT?

I BESEECH YOU, MAN! HELP ME SEARCH FOR THE BOAT!

CONTROL YOURSELF, MAN! I DON'T WANT TO HEAR YOUR BLUBBERING! WHAT ABOUT MOBY DICK?

MY SON, *MY BOY* WAS ON THAT BOAT!

AVAST, MAN. DO YOU THINK I'M INSANE TO BE LOOKING FOR A LOST CAUSE?

I'LL DO ANYTHING FOR YOU. PLEASE HELP ME!

THE DOG!

I'LL COVER YOUR EXPENSES FOR TWO DAYS. PLEASE HELP ME!

I'VE COME TWENTY THOUSAND MILES FOR THAT WHALE. DO YOU THINK I'LL *STOP NOW?*

NOW LEAVE!

HE'S A DEVIL! BLAST HIS ROTTEN HEART!

FROM THAT DAY, THE LONE, SINISTER FIGURE OF AHAB SITS IN A BASKET ON THE MAINMAST, HIS KEEN EYES SEARCHING THE WATERS FOR MILES AROUND.

AS HE WATCHES, THOUGHTS BEGIN TO TORTURE HIM . . .

THOSE MEN - THEY LOOKED AT ME WITH HATRED . . . WHAT TH'? CURSE THAT BIRD!

. . . AND A BIRD, SWOOPING DOWN, RIPS OFF HIS HAT.

ON DECK, ALL AHAB DOES IS TO PACE UP AND DOWN, UP AND DOWN -

STARBUCK!

SIR?

FOR FORTY YEARS NOW, I'VE BEEN WHALING . . . LIVING UNDER THE ACCURSED CODE OF SEA AND SKY . . . NEVER TRYING TO UNDERSTAND MY FELLOW BEINGS . . .

. . . NEVER REALIZING THAT I HAVE A WIFE AND CHILD, WIDOWED AND ORPHANED BY MY LUST FOR AN IDIOTIC QUEST. OH, HOW I WISH I COULD RETURN TO MY PEACEFUL HOME IN MY OLD AGE!

OH, CAPTAIN, CAPTAIN! TURN THE SHIP 'ROUND AND GO BACK!

WHAT DEVILISH, UNEARTHLY THING IS IT THAT CONTROLS MY WILL? I -- I CAN'T HELP IT. I CAN'T STOP . . . WE MUST GO ON!

YE--ES, SIR!

SUDDENLY, AHAB STIFFENS . . .

IT'S HERE! AT LAST

WHAT'S HERE?

MAN THE MAST HEADS! CALL ALL HANDS!

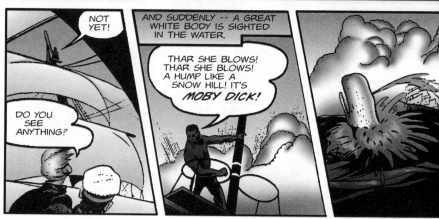

NOT YET!

DO YOU SEE ANYTHING?

AND SUDDENLY -- A GREAT WHITE BODY IS SIGHTED IN THE WATER.

THAR SHE BLOWS! THAR SHE BLOWS! A HUMP LIKE A SNOW HILL! IT'S *MOBY DICK!*

HE IS HEADING STRAIGHT FOR LEEWARD!

STAND BY THE BRACES. HARD DOWN HELM SHIVER HER! *BOATS! BOATS!*

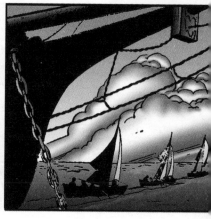

SAIL ON! DRIVE HIM OFF!

IS ALL SAFE?

AYE -- HARPOONS AND MEN!

HE'S OFF AGAIN . . . TO THE LEEWARD, SIR!

THEN WE SHALL GIVE CHASE!

AND DON'T FORGET, MEN. WHOEVER GETS HIM, GETS THAT COIN. AND IF IT BE ME, TEN TIMES THAT AMOUNT WILL BE DIVIDED AMONGST YE!

SOON AGAIN THE FAMILIAR CRY RESOUNDS, "THAR SHE BLOWS" -- *MOBY DICK!*

THAR SHE BREACHES!

IT CHALLENGES US AGAIN!

LIKE A RAGING INFERNO, THE WHALE AGAIN FIGHTS THE BOATS.

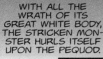

WITH ALL THE WRATH OF ITS GREAT WHITE BODY, THE STRICKEN MONSTER HURLS ITSELF UPON THE PEQUOD.

IT'S HEADIN' TOWARD THE SHIP!

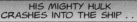

HIS MIGHTY HULK CRASHES INTO THE SHIP...

... AND SLOWLY THE PEQUOD SETTLES...

ONLY ONE PAIR OF ARMS RISES FROM THE WATER...

... AND CLINGING TO A BIT OF DEBRIS, A PROSTRATE FIGURE FLOATS FOR HOURS.

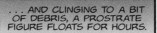

IT CAN'T BE ... NO, IT'S A MIRAGE - BUT IT MUST ... IT MUST BE - ... IT IS ... A SHIP! A SHIP!

THUS ISHMAEL IS THE LONE SURVIVOR OF THE ILL-FATED *PEQUOD*... RESCUED BY THE *RACHEL* AND ITS CAPTAIN, WHOSE PLEAS WERE UNHEEDED BY *AHAB!*

AND SO ENDS THE QUEST OF A MADMAN ... WHOSE MADNESS BROUGHT A VALIANT CREW TO ITS WATERY DOOM. NOW SMALL BIRDS FLY SCREAMING OVER THE ENDLESS EXPANSE OF OCEAN ... AND THE GREAT SHROUD OF THE SEA ROLLS ON AS IT HAS SINCE THE BEGINNING OF TIME ...

The End

MOBY DICK:
HERMAN MELVILLE

In 1850, Herman Melville wrote to his friend Richard Henry Dana (author of *Two Years Before the Mast*): "About the "whaling voyage"—I am half way in the work…It will be a strange sort of book, tho', I fear; blubber is blubber you know; tho' you may get oil out of it, the poetry runs as hard as sap from a frozen maple tree;—& to cook the thing up, one must needs throw in a little fancy, which from the nature of the thing, must be ungainly as the gambols of the whales themselves. Yet I mean to give the truth of the thing, spite of this."

In spite of these misgivings, Melville did indeed "give the truth of the thing." In 1851 his novel *Moby Dick, or the White Whale* appeared, and became then what it remains today, the definitive novel about the American whaling experience.

States, he taught school for a while before turning again to the sea, this time as a whaler. During his time in the whaling fleet he was first a bow-oarsman—one who, like *Moby Dick*'s narrator, Ishmael, pulls the oar in a whaleboat next after the harpooneer—and later a harpooneer himself.

In 1841, Melville sailed for the South Seas on the whaler *Acushnet*. Eighteen months into the voyage, he and a companion deserted the ship in the Marquesas Islands and lived there for a month among the natives. Melville left the island aboard an Australian trader, and made his way first to Tahiti and then to Honolulu. There, in 1843, he enlisted as a seaman aboard the U.S. Navy frigate *United States* (a ship that he later incorporated—and not flatteringly—into his novel *White-Jacket* as the U.S.S. *Neversink*.)

Melville's first novel, *Typee: A Peep at Polynesian Life*, appeared in 1846. It was loosely based upon his experiences after jumping ship in the Marquesas, and quickly proved popular. More novels followed over the course of his career—*Omoo, Mardi, Redburn, White-Jacket*, and *Billy Budd*, among others—but *Moby Dick*, the "romance of adventure" that appeared in 1851, is usually considered his masterpiece.

Herman Melville knew the ships and sailors he wrote about from personal experience. He was born on August 1, 1819, into a prominent New York family fallen on hard times, and went to sea for the first time while still in his teens, sailing as a cabin boy on a ship bound for Liverpool. Returning to the United

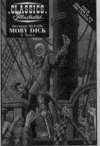

CLASSICS Illustrated
Herman Melville
MOBY DICK
& Notes

Ishmael The story's narrator. He's sailed on merchant ships before, and considers himself "something of a salt," but this is his first voyage on a whaler. He signs on board the *Pequod* for a three-hundredth lay, or share, of the profits of the cruise. "Ishmael" may not be his real name—in the first line of the book, he tells us "Call me Ishmael," as though that might be a nickname or a name assumed for the occasion. The name recalls the biblical Ishmael, a wanderer and outcast from the more settled tribes. Ishmael tells us that he is accustomed to go to sea as a cure for melancholy:

FORSOOTH, 'TIS GOOD OF YOU, QUEEQUEG. BUT YOU REALLY SHOULDN'T DO THIS FOR ME!

Whenever I find myself growing grim about the mouth; whenever it is a damp, drizzly November in my soul; whenever I find myself involuntarily pausing before coffin warehouses, and bringing up the rear of every funeral I meet; and especially whenever my hypos [gloomy thoughts] get such an upper hand of me, that it requires a strong moral principle to prevent me from deliberately stepping into the street, and methodically knocking people's hats off—then, I account it high time to get to sea as soon as I can.

Ishmael tells us very little more about himself, or about his earlier life ashore. Some things are implied, as when he says about going to sea as an ordinary sailor, "And at first, this sort of thing is unpleasant enough…especially if you come of an old established family in the land…. And more than all, if…you have been lording it as a country schoolmaster, making the tallest boys stand in awe of you." Ishmael never says outright that this description applies to him, and in fact it may not. It *does*, however, apply to Melville himself—suggesting that in some ways, at least, Ishmael is the character in the book most likely to speak to us with the author's voice.

Captain Ahab The one-legged captain of the whaling ship *Pequod*; Ahab is also known as "Old Thunder." In his earlier career, Ahab was a successful whaling captain, but the novel also hints at a past full of lurid incidents. As the old sailor Elijah says to Ishmael before the *Pequod* sails:

*What did they **tell** you about him?…nothing about that thing that happened to him off Cape Horn, long ago, when he lay like dead for three days and nights; nothing about that deadly skrimmage with the Spaniard afore the altar in Santa?—heard nothing about that, eh? Nothing about the silver calabash he spat into? And nothing about his losing his leg last voyage, according to the prophecy.*

Melville also suggests that Ahab is under a curse, perhaps having to do with his unlucky name. Captain Peleg, one of the *Pequod*'s owners, tells Ishmael: "Captain Ahab did not name himself. 'Twas a foolish ignorant whim of his crazy, widowed mother, who died when he was only a twelvemonth old. And yet the old squaw Tistig, at Gay-Head, said that the name would somehow prove prophetic." Since King Ahab, in the Bible, had his own prophet Elijah to contend with—a prophet who foretold the king's bloody downfall—Peleg's comments are ominous ones.

Ahab's appearance is striking: in addition to the missing leg, replaced by a peg leg made of whalebone, he has an impressive and mysterious scar:

Threading its way out from among his grey hairs, and continuing right down one side of his tawny scorched face and neck, till it disappeared in his clothing, you saw a slender rod-like mark, lividly whitish. It resembled that perpendicular seam sometimes made in the straight, lofty trunk of a great tree, when the upper lightning tearingly darts down it, and without wrenching a single twig, peels and grooves out the bark from top to bottom, ere running off into the soil, leaving the tree still greenly alive, but branded. Whether that mark was born with him, or

whether it was the scar left by some desperate wound, no one could certainly say...

Ahab himself claims to have received the scar from being literally struck by lightning during a storm at sea—but since he makes the claim while howling defiance at the elements in the middle of a typhoon, it's hard to know whether to believe him.

Ahab lost his leg in an encounter with the white whale, Moby Dick. The missing limb was replaced at sea by a peg leg carved out of whalebone, and Ahab is now determined to find and kill Moby Dick in order to get even—a goal he's kept hidden from the *Pequod*'s owners, who would naturally prefer their ship's captain to ignore vengeance and concentrate on filling the hold with barrels of whale oil.

Ishmael may be the narrator of Melville's book, but Ahab is its centerpiece. The one-legged captain of the *Pequod* is one of American fiction's unforgettable characters, a magnificent monomaniac whose quarrel really isn't with Moby Dick, but with God:

"Vengeance on a dumb brute!" cried Starbuck, *"that simply smote thee from blindest instinct! Madness! To be enraged with a dumb thing, Captain Ahab, seems blasphemous."*

YOU'RE THINKING OF THE OIL -- WHEREAS ONLY ONE THOUGHT TORTURES ME -- *MOBY DICK!*

"'Hark ye yet again, [Ahab replied]—*the little lower layer. All visible objects, man, are but pasteboard masks. But in each event—in the living act, the undoubted deed—there, some unknown but still reasoning thing puts forth the mouldings of its features from behind the unreasoning mask. If man will strike, strike through the mask! How can the prisoner reach outside except by thrusting through the wall? To me, the white whale is that wall, shoved near to me. Sometimes I think there's naught beyond. But 'tis enough.* He tasks me; he heaps me; I see in him outrageous strength with an inscrutable malice sinewing it. That inscrutable thing is chiefly what I hate, and be the white whale agent, or be the white whale principal, I will wreak that hate upon him. Talk not to me of blasphemy, man; I'd strike the sun if it insulted me.*"

To Ahab, the whale appears as a kind of living symbol, a "mask" worn by some greater power, that "unknown but still reasoning thing" which has taken his leg and blighted

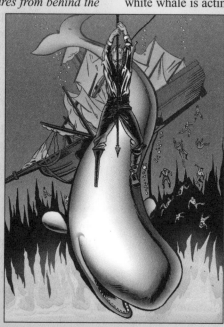

his existence. Ahab's God, as represented by the white whale, is not a kindly deity. The "inscrutable malice" belongs to the God who afflicted the Biblical Job—but Ahab is no Job, to bear his trials patiently. It doesn't matter to him whether the white whale is acting on behalf of the thing behind the mask—God—or acting deliberately and on its own behalf. Either way, he *will* strike back.

Moby Dick The huge white sperm whale that took Ahab's leg. Larger than life, supernaturally unkillable, Moby Dick is so plainly more than *just* a whale that generations of readers have argued over what exactly he stands for. Even Melville's own characters can't resist the urge to debate about it. Ahab regards the white whale as something like the physical mask of a malevolent God. Ishmael has his own thoughts, and in a chapter entitled "The Whiteness of the Whale," he goes over all the implications of the whale's peculiar color that he can think of, concluding that the negative meanings far outweigh the positive ones:

...for all these accumulated associations, with whatever is sweet, and honorable, and sublime, there yet lurks an elusive something in the innermost idea of this hue, which strikes more of a panic to the soul than that redness which affrights in blood.

This elusive quality it is, which causes the thought of whiteness, when divorced from more kindly associations and coupled with any object terrible in itself, to heighten that terror to the furthest bounds. Witness the white bear of the poles, and the white shark of the tropics; what but their smooth, flaky whiteness makes them the transcendent horrors that they are? That ghastly whiteness it is that imparts such an abhorrent mildness, even more loathsome than terrific, to the dumb gloating of their aspect.

"Bethink thee of the albatross, whence come those clouds of spiritual wonderment and pale dread, in which that white phantom sails in all imaginations? Not Coleridge [author of "The Rime of the Ancient Mariner"] *first threw that spell; but God's great, unflattering laureate, Nature.*

In the end, Ishmael sees in the whale not the active malice Ahab finds there, but an even more terrifying indifference. "Though in many of its aspects this visible world seems formed in love," he concludes, "the invisible spheres were formed in fright."

Queequeg Ishmael's best friend aboard the *Pequod*, and har-

pooneer in the whaleboat of Starbuck, the first mate. Queequeg is a South Sea Islander—not unusual, since many whaling ships picked up crewmen in the South Pacific, at

BUT QUEEQUEG DOESN'T WAIT FOR THE PLAUDITS OF THE CREW. - HE QUICKLY DISCARDS HIS CLOTHES AND DIVES OVERBOARD.

IS HE CRAZY? COME BACK, YOU!

Hawaii or other ports. Queequeg is a pagan, a (theoretically reformed) cannibal, and a headhunter. He's also courageous, charitable, good-humored, forgiving...in short, a better person, by the standards of *Moby Dick*'s Nantucket Island Quakers and Congregationalists, than they are themselves. As a skilled harpooneer, he signs on to the *Pequod* for a seventieth lay.

Three times Queequeg rescues a fellow-sailor from drowning: once on the ship from New Bedford to Nantucket; again, when he cuts Tashtego free of the sinking head of the slaughtered sperm whale; and finally, after the sinking of the *Pequod*, when his empty coffin provides the piece of wreckage to which Ishmael clings and is saved. Queequeg embodies the support and fellowship which stands between humanity and a malicious or indifferent nature.

Tashtego Harpooneer in the whaleboat of Stubb, the *Pequod*'s second mate. Tashtego is a Native American from the Gay Head area of Martha's Vineyard. He's last glimpsed nailing the *Pequod*'s colors to her mast as she sinks:

But as the last whelmings [floating pieces of broken wreckage] poured themselves over the sunken head of the Indian at the mainmast, leaving a few inches of the erect spar yet visible, together with long streaming yards of the flag, which calmly undulated, with ironical coincidings, over the

Multicultural Whaling

Although the American whaling industry of the nineteenth century was based in New England, and although the captains and mates of the ships still came from the old Nantucket and New Bedford whaling families, the ships' crews were as varied in reality as the *Pequod*'s was in fiction. Whaling was a hard life, and the pay, based on shares of a voyage's profits, was nothing to make a man rich—as a British whaling song of the period put it, "we've signed away four years of our lives, and earned about three pounds ten." Melville speaks of ships returning from a four-year voyage with only four barrels of oil, and he devotes an entire chapter to the question of whether the depredations of the whaleships had created a marked decrease in the whale population. Increasingly, as the century drew on, Yankee boys seeking work found opportunities for better employment in the mills, on the railroads, and in the expanding West. But there were still sailors willing to endure hard labor and harsh conditions in the hopes of earning a share of the profits on a lucky voyage.

The Native Americans of Nantucket and Martha's Vineyard had long worked on the whaling ships—

Tashtego would never have seemed an oddity. Nor, as time passed, would have Queequeg or Daggoo. The men of the whaling crews came from the Azores and Cape Verde Islands, from Europe and South America, and from the South Sea Islands. American Midwesterners and ex-slaves in need of work (as well as free-born northern African-Americans) also signed on board for the three and four year voyages. Some of these non-Yankee whalers achieved fame in their chosen profession. For example, the toggle iron—a more efficient harpoon than the older spear-headed version—was invented in 1848 by an African-American whaler named Lewis Temple, and a statue in his honor stands in New Bedford today.

destroying billows they almost touched;—at that instant a red arm and a hammer hovered backwardly uplifted in the open air, in the act of nailing the flag faster and yet faster to the subsiding spar.

As Tashtego does so, a sky-hawk becomes entangled in the sodden flag and sinks with the ship, "which, like Satan, would not sink to hell till she had dragged a living part of heaven along with her, and helmeted herself with it."

Daggoo   Daggoo, a native of Africa, is the harpooneer for Flask, the third mate. His great height—six-foot-five inches—and his dignified bearing make a double contrast with Flask's diminutive stature and half-sinister comic behavior.

Fedallah   Ahab's harpooneer, and one of a boat-crew of similar characters, whom Ishmael glimpses coming aboard in the early morning fog just before the *Pequod*'s departure. Nobody sees them until the first time Ahab's whaleboat is lowered, and it's implied that they live somewhere in the ship's hold. Fedallah and his mates are sinister fellows, connected in some way with Ahab's obsession. Flask and Stubb speculate that Fedallah may be the devil himself, with whom Ahab has struck some kind of unholy bargain. Ishmael, more rationally, thinks that Ahab must have smuggled Fedallah and his boat-crew aboard in order to avoid alarming the ship's owners, who might have objected to their crip-

pled captain joining the whale-chase in person.

Starbuck   First mate of the *Pequod*. "Starbuck" was a well-known family name in Nantucket and New Bedford (for that matter, so was "Coffin", the name of the proprietor of *Moby Dick*'s Spouter Inn.) Members of the Starbuck family served as mates and captains on whaling ships from the late 1700s on into the nineteenth century. Melville's Starbuck is prudent, rather than rash and impulsive, saying "'I will have no man in my boat…who is not afraid of a whale." He is a good man, and one

THERE HE LIES, SLEEPING. OH LORD, IF ONLY I HAD THE COURAGE TO WREST THE POWER FROM HIS LIVING HANDS!

who sees that Ahab's mad pursuit of vengeance can only end in disaster, but his courage is physical rather than moral.

Starbuck is overpowered in the end by Ahab's stronger will. He proves unwilling to stop Ahab by means of murder or mutiny, and isn't imaginative enough to think of alternatives.

Stubb   Second mate of the *Pequod*. A calm, matter-of-fact sort of man, more materialistic than philosophical—he regards the whale as a source of food (that is, as a physical resource) rather than a source of meaning. He stands in contrast to Starbuck and Flask.

Flask Third mate of the *Pequod*. A short, energetic man, one who hunts and kills whales with great enthusiasm for his work, but without feeling any "sense of reverence for the many marvels of their majestic bulk and mystic ways." He has a rough, aggressive sense of humor, and—though he is himself the most junior of the *Pequod*'s three mates—he will tease or bully people like Pip the cabin boy, who happen to be under his authority.

Point of View and Narrative Voice

Moby Dick begins, at least, as a first-person novel, a tale told by some real or fictional speaker (the "I" of the story). Ishmael plays the part admirably: he's a thoughtful narrator with a healthy sense of humor. But before the *Pequod*'s story is done, the limits of first-person point of view will have been strained to the breaking point—and possibly beyond.

One of the limits of first-person narration is that the narrator can only describe things that he is personally aware of. He can't tell the inner thoughts of others, or describe any action that he himself did not observe or that he could not reasonably have been told. Yet Ishmael records Ahab's words and thoughts when the captain is alone, and gives us the details of activities on other boats. To take one example: where was Ishmael standing on the occasion when Captain Ahab pointed a musket at Starbuck, while Ahab and the first mate were alone in the captain's cabin? Sometimes, also, the

BUT CONSIDER THE OWNERS -- AND THE LIVES OF THE MEN ON THIS VESSEL!

YOU THINK OF THEM! -- BUT MIND YOU, AS THERE IS ONE GOD RULING THIS EARTH, THERE IS ONE CAPTAIN OF THE PEQUOD -- AND THAT IS *ME* . . . AHAB! NOW, *GET OUT!*

story drops into dramatic, almost Shakespearean, form, with entire chapters told with dialogue and stage directions (and chapter heads like *Enter Ahab: to him, Stubb*), and with various characters giving soliloquies. And finally, Ishmael's narrative voice sometimes becomes hard to distinguish from the voice of Herman Melville, speaking directly to the reader about the natural history of whales, world history and geography, and philosophy.

These slips and shifts in point of view aren't the result of carelessness or clumsy writing; there are too many of them, and things like the soliloquies and dramatic passages aren't written that way by accident. The expansion of Ishmael's viewpoint to become that of the ship's crew in general makes more sense after looking at the physical dimensions and layout of a whaling ship—small (under a hundred feet in length) and cramped enough that physical isolation would be almost impossible. Mostly, though, Melville seems to have employed the sort of mixed form he used for *Moby Dick* because he didn't want to be confined by the narrow boundaries of any narrative voice. *Moby Dick* is at least three books rolled into one—the story of the friendship between Ishmael and Queequeg, the story of Captain Ahab's wrath against God, and a long non-fiction essay on commercial whaling in the mid-nineteenth century—and Melville feels free to alter his style and point of view according to which one he is dealing with at the moment.

THE BLUBBER IS THEN REMOVED TO THE BLUBBER ROOM, AND COILED BY MANY HANDS.

"A Dead Whale or a Stove Boat!": the American Whaling Industry

In the years before kerosene and plastic became common, whale products had many uses. The spermaceti from the head, or case, of the sperm whale would be made into candles; the whale's fat, or blubber, yielded a fine, pure oil, valuable both for lighting and for oiling delicate machinery. The whalebone,

or baleen, from the mouth of the right whale and other plankton-eating whales was used in manufacturing articles that required a combination of stiffness and flexibility (corset stays, for example, and buggy whips). The ambergris from the whale's intestines was used in making fine perfumes.

The New England whaling industry began in the mid-1600s with off-shore whaling, the pursuit of whales in small boats launched from the shore. Nantucket—a low sandy island rising out of the Atlantic Ocean off Massachusetts—was the first major whaling center. From about 1830 onward, however, New Bedford, Massachusetts, served as the country's most important whaling port. When Ishmael decides to go from New Bedford to Nantucket in order to sign aboard a whaler, in a sense he is taking a deliberate step backward in time:

For my mind was made up to sail in none other than a Nantucket craft, because there was a fine, boisterous something about everything connected with that famous old island, which amazingly pleased me. Besides, though New Bedford has of late been gradually monopolizing the business of whaling, and though in this matter poor old Nantucket is now very much behind her, yet Nantucket was her great original—the Tyre of this

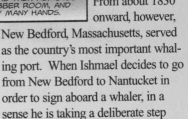

Carthage;— the place where the first dead American whale was stranded. Where else but Nantucket did those aboriginal whalemen, the Red-men, first sally out in canoes to give chase to the Leviathan? And where but from Nantucket, too, did that first adventurous little sloop put forth, partly laden with imported cobblestones—so goes the story—to throw at the whales, in order to discover when they were nigh enough to risk a harpoon from the bowsprit?"

At first the New England whale hunters took only those whales which

IT'S A SPERM WHALE THIS TIME!

showed up in the waters offshore. Later on, as the whale population diminished and the demand for whale products rose, whaling ships went hunting in the Arctic and (like the *Pequod*) in the South Seas. These voyages could last for three or four years at a time.

The two main species of whale hunted in the nineteenth century were the right whale and the sperm whale. The right whale, in particular, took its name from those characteristics which first made it, from the mariners' point of view, the "right" whale to hunt: it was a slow enough swimmer for the oar-driven chase boats to catch it; and once killed, it floated rather than sank.

Both species also grew to large, and therefore profitable, sizes: Modern sperm whales can grow to a length of sixty feet (for a male) and forty feet (for a female). Melville describes the sperm whales of his own day as being eighty to ninety feet long, but this may be a dramatic exaggeration.

Throughout most of the nineteenth century whales were hunted and killed in the way Herman Melville describes so vividly in *Moby Dick*: pursued by sailors in oar-driven whaleboats, then struck by harpoons and, ultimately, killed by driving a whaling lance down into the lungs directly behind the blowhole. All this was done at close range, and was powered by human muscle, at considerable risk to the hunters.

Whaling changed dramatically with the introduction of engine-powered chase boats, along with explosive harpoons and air pumps to inflate and float the carcasses. No longer did the whalers have to confine themselves to the slower-moving whales, or to those whales whose bodies remained afloat after they were killed. Whale populations already greatly reduced by hunting began to decline even more sharply than before. The *Charles W. Morgan*, an old-style sail powered whaling ship, took a lifetime total of 60,000 barrels of oil in thirty-seven voyages during an active career of 80 years. In the 1960s a single factory ship assisted by twelve catcher boats took 80,000 barrels of oil in a single 112-day season off Antarctica.

For a "living history" approach to the American whaling industry, there's Mystic Seaport in Mystic, Connecticut, where the former whaling ship *Charles W. Morgan* has been restored as a floating museum exhibit. Museum staff members are very knowledgeable about both Herman Melville and whaling in general. Mary K. Bercaw Edwards, Ph. D., in particular, was helpful in the writing of this essay—any errors in it are my fault, not hers.

Themes

"Canst Thou Draw out Leviathan with an Hook?"—Job 41:1

God's question to Job is clearly meant to be answered "No"—but Job wasn't a New England whale fisherman.

"Shall I send you a fin of the Whale by way of a specimen mouthful? Melville wrote in late June of 1851 to his friend Nathaniel Hawthorne (author of **The Scarlet Letter**.) "The tail is not yet cooked—though the hell-fire in which the whole book is broiled might not unreasonably have cooked it all ere this. This is the book's motto (the secret one),—Ego non baptiso te in nomine—but make out the rest yourself."

The "secret motto" of Melville's book doesn't stay a secret forever. Ahab speaks it in its entirety while he is forging his second harpoon: *Ego non baptiso te in nomine patris, sed in nomine diaboli* (I do not baptize thee in the name of the father, but in the name of the devil). More than once, Ahab's behavior smacks of diabolism in a way that, for example, Queequeg's idol-worshipping does not. Consider, first, the ceremony in which Ahab forces the *Pequod*'s crew to take an oath to destroy Moby Dick. He calls the crew together on the ship's quarter-deck at sunset, and after working them up into a frenzy of enthusiasm, promises a gold doubloon to the sailor who first sights the white whale. Then he makes his vow of revenge in terms full of violence and ill omen:

"Aye, aye! it was that accursed white whale that razed me; made a poor pegging lubber of me for ever and a day!" Then tossing out both arms, with measureless imprecations he shouted out: "Aye, aye! and I'll chase him round Good Hope, and round the Horn, and round the Norway Maelstrom, and round perdition's flames before I give him up. And this is what ye have shipped for, men! to chase the white whale on both sides of the land, and over all sides of earth, till he spouts black blood and rolls fin out."

What follows is almost a blasphemous parody of a religious ritual. First the "great measure" of grog is distributed among the crew, who drink from a pewter goblet passed from hand to hand in a kind of mock communion. Then Ahab orders the harpooneers to remove the wooden shafts from their harpoons, and has them turn the three-foot long iron barbs over so that the hollow socket-ends (where the shafts had previously been) are now upward. Filling the makeshift cups with grog, he forces the *Pequod*'s mates and their har-

pooneers to drink in their turn, and to join him in his vow:

"Now, three to three, ye stand. Commend the murderous chalices! Bestow them, ye who are now made parties to this indissoluble league... the deed is done! Yon ratifying sun now waits to sit upon it. Drink, ye harpooneers! drink and swear, ye men that man the deathful whale-boat's bow—Death to Moby Dick! God hunt us all, if we do not hunt Moby Dick to his death!"

(Ahab should know better than to say things like that: the sea has a way of hearing such rash promises,

and of making sure that a person keeps them. Another "wild legend" of the southern seas is that of the Flying Dutchman, a captain who swore that he would never stop trying to make it around Cape Horn, no matter how long it took. He would "be damned" if he did. This was, of course, a direct affront to God, and he's been trying to make it around the Horn ever since.)

Later, when Ahab has the ship's blacksmith make him a special harpoon, he once again employs a ritual of his own devising:

...as the blacksmith was about giving the barbs their final heat, prior to tempering them, he cried to Ahab to place the water-cask near [to quench the metal].

"No, no—no water for that; I want it of the true death-temper. Ahoy, there! Tashtego, Queequeg, Daggoo! What say ye, pagans! Will ye give me as much blood as will cover this barb?" holding it high up. A cluster of dark nods replied, Yes. Three punctures were made in the heathen flesh, and the White Whale's barbs were then tempered.

"Ego non baptizo te in nomine patris, sed in nomine diaboli!" deliriously howled Ahab, as the malignant iron scorchingly devoured the baptismal blood.

The harpoon itself—wound up from twelve pure strands of iron, the iron taken from used horseshoe nails (the hardest iron, we are told, a blacksmith knows), and tipped with a point forged from Ahab's razors with which he had daily touched his own skin, welded together by a sinner-smith who had come to sea seeking death, tempered in the blood of the ship's non-Christian harpooneers, and baptized in the name of the Devil—is clearly more than a simple spear for killing an ordinary (if large) whale. When Ahab got mad at God, he didn't mess around.

Part of the irony in *Moby Dick* is that it's a "civilized" Western man who's doing all this. The "heathen" harpooneers whom he involves in his rituals are, on their own terms and in their own time, better behaved, saner, and more moral than he is. In the long run it's Ahab who destroys them, rather than the other way around. He also destroys his ship, which itself belongs in part to the "heathen" side of things: the name *Pequod* is a reference to the Pequot tribe, a group of Native Americans eventually wiped out by the early New England settlers.

To balance out the diabolism, *Moby Dick* is heavy with biblical references and symbolism. Images of water and baptism abound. In addition to the book's repeated near-drownings and sudden rescues, we have the ocean itself as a source of meaning and significance. Ishmael spends his time at the masthead, when he should be on the lookout for whales, wondering what the ocean means. Sometimes he sees it as the source of all life and inspiration. Sometimes he sees it as an endless unmarked graveyard for the nameless dead. Sometimes it's a spiritual world, and at others a meaningless confusion of elemental power. (Not surprisingly, Ishmael is so preoccupied with his philosophical musings that he fails to spot any whales.)

Melville also uses the old New England custom of giving biblical names: there's Ahab himself, a "crowned king" in the bible, but an ill-omened one, and Ishmael the wanderer, and old Elijah, Ahab's prophet of doom. Even the name of a ship can be made to carry a biblical allusion. The sorrowful *Rachel*—the ship which Ahab refuses to help search for her missing crewmen, and which ultimately rescues Ishmael—calls to mind Matthew 2:18: "In Rama was there a voice heard, lamentation, and weeping, and great mourning, Rachel weeping for her children, and would not be comforted, because they are not."

Melville also makes repeated references to Jonah, who was punished for refusing to obey God's command by being imprisoned in the belly of a whale, and to Job, who bore up patiently under affliction. But these biblical stories and characters do not serve Ahab as models for behavior; instead, he stands in stark contrast to them. During the typhoon near the end of the book he addresses the lightning as though it were itself a deity:

AYE, AYE, MEN. MARK IT WELL. THE WHITE FLAME LEADS US TO THE *WHITE WHALE!*

Oh, thou clear spirit of clear fire, whom on these seas I as Persian [a fire-worshiper, like his own harpooneer Fedallah] *once did worship, till in the sacramental act so burned by thee, that to this hour I bear the scar; I now know thee, thou clear spirit, and I know that thy right worship is defiance. To neither love nor reverence wilt thou be kind; and e'en for hate thou canst but kill; and all are killed…Come in thy lowest form of love, and I will kneel and kiss thee; but at thy highest, come as mere supernal power; and though thou launchest navies of full-freighted worlds, there's that in here [in Ahab himself] that still remains indifferent. Oh, thou clear spirit, of thy fire thou madest me, and like a true child of fire, I breathe it back to thee.*

Compared to stuff like this, Queequeg's worship of his idol, Yojo, back in New Bedford, seems tame— "innocent," as Ishmael calls it at the time—and Yojo certainly seems to be a kinder and more well-meaning deity than Ahab's "spirit of clear fire." The book turns all the normal expectations of Melville's original Victorian readers inside out. It makes the book's dark-skinned pagans and cannibals (especially Queequeg) into kind and charitable figures, while making the white Christians into ineffectual figures (like Starbuck) or into demonic forces of destruction (like Ahab). Considering what sort of games Melville was up to, fictionally speaking, it's no wonder that he concluded his 1851 remarks to Nathaniel Hawthorne with "I have written a wicked book, and feel spotless as the lamb."

The Sinking of the Whaleship Essex

Melville based *Moby Dick* in large part on his own experiences at sea. In addition, he did research to increase the realism of the story—his assertion that he drew on "wild legends" for his material doesn't keep the novel from being an authentic picture of life and work aboard an American whaling ship when the industry was at its height. Even the dramatic climax of the novel, the destruction of the *Pequod* by the wounded and enraged Moby Dick, has a firm basis in fact (as Melville is careful to foreshadow in some detail long before Moby Dick is ever sighted). Whales could and frequently did smash up the smaller, oar-powered boats that were sent out to chase and kill them—and on one

famous occasion the whaling ship itself was stove in and sunk by a whale's attack.

In 1819 (thirty-two years before Melville published his novel), the whaling ship *Essex* left New England on what would be her final cruise. She carried a crew of twnty-one men, mostly from Nantucket. Among them was Owen Chase, the First Mate, who later gave an account of the disaster that overtook the *Essex* after she had reached the whaling area in the South Pacific known as the Offshore Ground.

I observed a very large spermaceti whale, as well as I could judge, about eighty-five feet in length; he broke water about twenty rods off our weather-bow [about 330 feet away, about 45 degrees forward of the ship on the side the wind was blowing from] *and was lying quietly, with his head in a direction for the ship. He spouted two or three times, and then disappeared. In less than two or three seconds he came up again, about the length of the ship* [about 87 feet] *off, and made directly for us, at the rate of about three knots* [three nautical miles per hour]... *I involuntarily ordered the boy at the helm to put it hard up* [turn into the direction the whale was coming from, to present the smallest aspect; the same maneuver is standard today in the event of torpedo attack]; *intending to sheer off and avoid him. The words were scarcely out of my mouth, before he came down upon us with full speed, and struck the ship with his head, just forward of the fore-chains* [the point where the chains holding the bowsprit in place are attached, a short way behind the stem post, but with the side of the ship still curved]; *he gave us such an appalling and tremendous jar, as nearly threw us all on our faces.... I again discovered the whale, apparently in convulsions, on the top of the water, about one hundred rods to leeward* [a little over sixteen hundred feet away, on the opposite side of the ship, the direction away from the wind]. *He was enveloped in the foam of the sea, that his continual and violent thrashing about in the water had created around him, and I could distinctly see him smite his jaws together as if distracted with rage and fury.... I was aroused with the cry of a man at the hatchway, "here he is—he is making for us again." I turned around, and saw him about one hundred rods directly ahead of us* [1650 feet, or close to a third of a mile], *coming down apparently with twice his ordinary speed, and to me at that moment, it appeared with tenfold fury and vengeance in his aspect. The surf flew in all directions about him, and his course towards us was marked by a white foam of a rod in width, which he made with the continual violent thrashing of his tail; his head was about half out of water, and in that way he came upon, and again struck the ship...I should judge the speed of the ship to have been at this time about three knots, and that of the whale about six. He struck her to windward, directly under the cat-head* [the place where the anchors are stowed], *and completely stove in* [crushed] *her bows.*

HIS MIGHTY HULK CRASHES INTO THE SHIP ...

The *Essex* sank. Owen Chase and the other members of her crew spent over three months adrift in their open whaleboats, eventually resorting to cannibalism before being rescued. Their story became well-known in the whaling fleet. During Herman Melville's own whaling days, he met and spoke with Owen Chase's son; and later, Melville acquired a copy of Owen Chase's published account, from which he quoted liberally in *Moby Dick*.

•What do you think is the significance of Ahab's mysterious scar, and why should there be a debate over whether he was born with it, or acquired it later in life? If the scar—a mark that sets him apart as having been, in some way, "struck by lightning"—has not always been a part of him, does this add to the weight of Ahab's quarrel with God, or take away from it?

•How are Ishmael and Ahab alike, and how are they different? Do they have any ideas or concerns in common? Why might Melville have chosen Ishmael as his main narrator for telling Ahab's story?

•Do you find Ahab's desire to "strike through the mask," and his single-minded pursuit of the white whale, to be admirable, appalling, or a mixture of both? Why?

•If the three mates (Starbuck, Stubb, and Flask) had survived the voyage of the *Pequod*, what kind of captains would they have made in their own ships? Which one of them would you rather have sailed with, and why?

•Which is better, morally speaking: to pursue, as Ahab does, a single whale out of a desire for vengeance, but without regard for the consequences of that pursuit to anyone else; or to kill whales as Flask does, as though "the wondrous whale was but a species of magnified mouse, or at least water-rat, requiring only a little circumvention and some small application of time and trouble in order to kill and boil?"

•What might Starbuck have done, other than killing Ahab, to stop him from destroying the *Pequod* and her crew? Given that the first mate clearly foresees the disaster that's coming, how much does his failure to act make him responsible for it?

About the Essayist:

Debra Doyle holds a Ph.D. from the University of Pennsylvania, and has taught at Penn, Villanova, and the University of New Hampshire. With her husband James Macdonald, Dr. Doyle is the author of adult and young adult fantasy and science fiction, including the popular Mageworld series.